P9-DNM-705

LEGO NINJAGO
Masters of Spinjitzu

ATTACK OF THE NINDROIDS

ADAPTED BY KATE HOWARD

SCHOLASTIC INC.

ISBN 978-0-545-64390-0

LEGO, the LEGO logo, the Brick and Knob configurations and the
Minifigure are trademarks of the LEGO Group. © 2014 The LEGO Group.
Produced by Scholastic Inc. under license from the LEGO Group.
Published by Scholastic Inc. SCHOLASTIC and associated logos are
trademarks and/or registered trademarks of Scholastic Inc.

10 9 8 7 6 5 4 3 2 1   14 15 16 17 18 19/0
Printed in the U.S.A.   40
First printing, April 2014

SCHOOL'S OUT

"Recess!" Cole cheered. "My favorite."

The teachers at Wu's Youth Academy hurried to the break room.

"All right, who took my pudding?" Jay growled. "It had my name on it."

Cole slurped up the last bite. "I didn't see 'motormouth' on it."

"I'm telling the headmaster," Jay whined.

Sensei Wu looked up from his tea. "Leave me out of it. I'm on break, too."

"Is anyone else mad Lloyd gets to fly around accepting awards while we're stuck here being teachers?" Jay asked.

Cole, Jay, Zane, and Kai had once been great ninja warriors. But there were no more enemies to fight. Lloyd, the Golden Ninja, had defeated the Overlord. The age of the ninja had come to an end.

"Did you guys hear the news?" asked Kai's sister, Nya, hurrying into the room.

"There's trouble?" Kai guessed.

"Danger?" Jay said.

"An emergency?" Zane hoped.

"No," Nya said. "We're going on a field trip to Borg Industries!"

FIELD TRIP!

The students and teachers piled into the school bus. When they arrived in New Ninjago City, everyone stared out the windows. Hover cars flew by. The city was filled with neon lights.

Cyrus Borg had invented many devices that had transformed old Ninjago City into a city of the future.

A droid welcomed them to Borg Industries. "I'm Pixal," she said. "Cyrus Borg's Primary Interactive Xternal Assistant Life-form." Pixal turned to Zane. "What does 'Zane' stand for?"

Zane stood tall. "Freedom — and courage in the face of all who threaten Ninjago."

"She means your name." Jay laughed.

"I guess I'm just 'Zane,'" said Zane. Like Pixal, he was a robot.

"Permission to scan?" Pixal asked Zane.

Zane didn't know what that meant. But he felt important. "Uh . . . permission granted?"

Pixal's eyes scanned Zane's body. Then she said, "Mr. Borg would like to see the ninja on the hundredth floor."

MEET CYRUS BORG

The elevator doors opened into Cyrus Borg's office. "I would have guessed ninja would sneak in a window, not use the elevator," the inventor said.

"Isn't this the same place where the Overlord was destroyed?" asked Kai.

"Yes," said Borg. "What better way to send a message that we won't cower to anyone?"

"I wanted to give you a gift," Borg said.

"A gift?" Cole looked excited. "We won't say no to that. It wouldn't happen to be a cake, would it?"

Cyrus Borg pulled a sheet off a golden statue.

"Wow," Kai said slowly. "A statue . . . of yourself."

A MYSTERIOUS MISSION

The inventor pulled Kai to one side. *"Please, protect them with your life!* All of Ninjago depends on it!"

Kai didn't understand. "Protect? Protect what?"

"I should never have built here," Borg whispered. "You must go. . . . *He is listening*!"

"I'm sorry to cut this short," Borg told the others. "I hope you can show yourselves out."

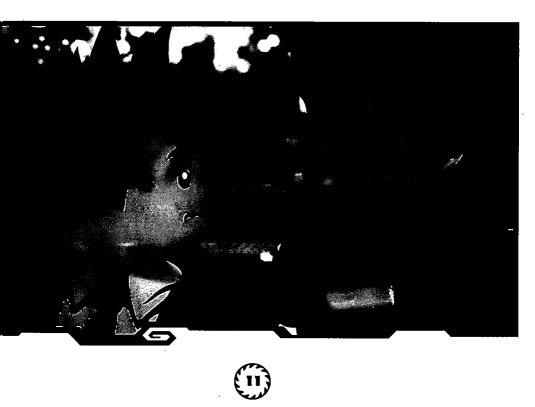

"Guys, something weird is up with Borg," Kai said as they carried the statue into the elevator. "He was acting scared. He said we had to protect 'them' with our lives."

"Them?" Cole asked. "Who?"

"I dunno, but —" Just then, the statue tipped onto the floor and cracked open.

"There's something inside!" Zane said.

Cole picked up ninja outfits hidden inside the statue. "Why would Cyrus Borg give us new ninja outfits?"

Kai held up four strange weapons. "And what exactly are these?"

Suddenly, the elevator stopped. *"TECHNO WEAPONS LOCATED!!!!!"* a computer voice announced. *"Please drop the Techno-Blades."*

"Guys!" Kai yelled. "These must be the Techno-Blades. We have to protect them with our lives."

"Have it your way. Good-bye," the computer said.

A moment later, the computer released the elevator brakes. The elevator plummeted toward the ground!

Kai flipped up and slammed his feet into the top of the elevator. He had opened the escape hatch! "Going up?"

Cole, Jay, and Zane knew what they had to do. *"NINJAAAA-GO!"*

The four ninja used Spinjitzu to leap to safety.

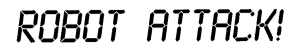

ROBOT ATTACK!

Meanwhile, Pixal was showing Nya, Sensei Wu, and their students around Borg Industries. Suddenly, Pixal's eyes began to glow red. "This will be the end of your tour."

Flash! Lasers fired at the group. Sensei Wu and Nya fought back.

Something evil was controlling the machines inside Borg Industries!

Luckily, the ninja were ready for action.

"Gotta say it," Jay said. "I love the new threads."

Suddenly, evil security robots surrounded them, firing lasers.

"Oh, yeah?" Kai said. He aimed his new Techno-Blade at the robots. "Two can play at this game. *Hi-yah!*"

But nothing happened. The Techno-Blade didn't work!

Kai shook it. "What's with these things? How do we turn them on?"

The security guards fired again. A blast shattered the window. The ninja fell through and plunged toward the ground!

"Hold on!" Cole yelled to the others. He was holding a fire hose! The ninja swung through the air together.

"Ready to crash the party, boys?" Cole asked. They smacked into a window. *Splat!*

The four ninja slid down the side of the building onto a window-cleaning platform.

RETURN OF
THE OVERLORD?

The ninja knew they had to figure out who was trying to get the Techno Weapons. Kai thought it was the evil Overlord.

"But how?" Cole said. "We all saw Lloyd defeat him."

Zane nodded. "Defeat, yes. But can he be destroyed?"

A Hover-Copter zoomed toward them.

"I don't know," Jay said. "But *we* can!"

"Cole, throw me!" Zane yelled.

Cole threw Zane onto the Hover-Copter. Zane landed on top and slammed his Techno-Blade into the cockpit.

The Blade lit up. White lightning glowed all around the Hover-Copter. Now it was a Ninja-Copter!

"The Blade hacked the Hover-Copter's system," Jay cried. "Zane controls it!"

Zane zoomed over to pick up Cole, Kai, and Jay. The ninja had students to rescue!

The Ninja-Copter hovered outside Borg Industries. Inside, their students were still under attack. The Ninja-Copter's lasers fired through the windows.

The students cheered. They were safe!

Soon the students were back on the school bus.

Kai turned to Nya. "Get to the Academy as fast as you can, sis. Find Lloyd. We need the Golden Ninja."

"What about you guys?" Nya asked.

"We must stay to protect the people," said Sensei Wu.

HACK ATTACK!

The four ninja and Sensei Wu huddled together. "These Techno-Blades can hack into their systems," Kai said.

Jay grinned. "Whaddaya say we do a li'l Hack Attack?"

"Zane, Kai — you take to the skies. I want Cole and Jay on the ground. I'll do what I can for the people," said Sensei Wu.

"Ninjaaa-go!" the four ninja cheered.

Zane steered his Ninja-Copter into the sky. Kai rode on top. "Oh, I want *that*!"

Kai jumped onto a jet fighter and slammed his Techno-Blade into it. Fire ripped across it, and it turned into a Kai-Fighter!

Suddenly, a hologram of Cyrus Borg appeared. Borg told Kai that the ninja needed to get the Techno-Blades out of the city or the Overlord would destroy them.

New Ninjago City was in grave danger. The ninja were under attack! Dozens of armed robots were on their trail.

Jay flipped toward an evil security tank. He jammed his Techno-Blade into it. Blue lightning shot over it. Now the tank was Jay's!

Nearby, Cole swung onto a Security Mech. He slammed into it with his Techno-Blade. It turned jet black. Cole was in control!

"We have to get the Techno-Blades out of the city," Kai told the other ninja.

"But what about Sensei?" Zane asked. Sensei Wu had been helping the people of New Ninjago City escape.

"I'll pick him up," Kai said.

But Sensei Wu was surrounded by hostile robots!

Suddenly, a golden blast blew everyone back. It was Lloyd, the Golden Ninja!

Evil laughter filled the air. "Golden Ninja. We meet again."

"Overlord," Lloyd said. "I defeated you once; I'll defeat you again."

"Oh, I don't want to fight," the Overlord said. "I just want your power!"

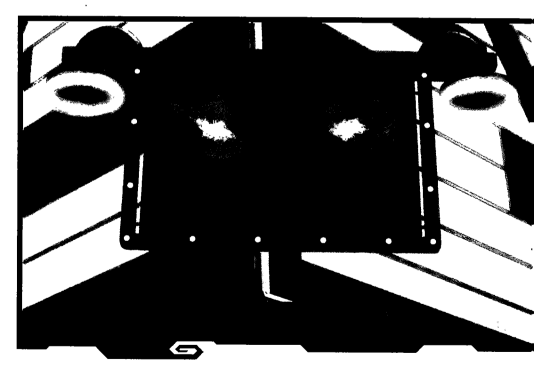

CHAPTER 5

A DARING PLAN

"Lloyd, your power is making him stronger," Sensei Wu cried.

"We need to get you and the Techno-Blades out of the city," Kai added.

"I have an idea," Sensei Wu said quietly. "Listen closely. . . ."

A moment later, the ninja all spun to their vehicles. *"Ninjaaaa-go!"*

Sensei Wu dashed across the rooftops of New Ninjago City. He was carrying a bundle covered in cloth.

"The sensei has the Techno-Blades!" the Overlord's voice boomed.

In no time, Sensei Wu was surrounded by Hover-Copters. He opened his bundle. It was empty! Sensei's plan had worked.

The other ninja zoomed out of New Ninjago City in their new vehicles. They had escaped with the Techno-Blades!

"We have to go back for Sensei," Lloyd said.

Kai nodded. "We will. When you are safe."

"The Overlord wants these weapons," Cole told Lloyd. "But he also wants you."

"We will come back to New Ninjago City," Zane added. "And when we do, we'll be ready."

Back in New Ninjago City, evil had taken over. "The city is ours," the Overlord said. "It's time we create our own ninja."

Pixal loaded a scan of Zane into the computers. "Upgrade complete." Borg's factory began to produce hundreds of ninja droids — *nindroids*!

Cole, Jay, Kai, Zane, and Lloyd were about to face some serious competition.